TRACY LOVES RAY

Written by Theresa Child

Inspired by the song "Tracy Loves Ray" by Jay Hitt

Additional storyline created by Glenn Child

Copyright © 2008 Child Family Publishing LLC
All rights reserved.

Cover Design: Brett Mason
www.pittsburghartists.com
click on ARTISTS
click on BRETT MASON

ISBN: 1-4392-0507-8
ISBN-13: 9781439205075

Visit www.booksurge.com to order additional copies.

*For creative people everywhere
who find inspiration in everyday life
and share it with others.*

ACKNOWLEDGEMENTS

I never wanted to be a writer. I never planned on writing a book and I certainly never thought that I would have the opportunity to thank everyone who helped me grow into who I am today in such a public way. So, please bear with me while I make the most of this unique opportunity.

First, I would like to thank my mother and father, Sally and Glenn Child. Not only was this project my father's baby, but their example of marriage made it easy to write about Tracy and Ray's love story. I also want to thank my brother, Cary. Although he is wise beyond his thirty some years, he'll always be my cute, little brother. It has been an honor to watch him grow and teach me how to grow as well. He is also the father of one of the most important people in my life, my nephew, Coleman. Before Cole was born, I had experienced all kinds of love, love for my family, love for my friends and even romantic love. But I had never experienced instant love. Whether we're spending a week together at Vacation Bible School, baking cookies, or just playing in the park, every moment with Cole is simple and genuine. I would be remiss if I didn't mention Cole's mother, Rebecca (and her family). Even though she and Cary are no longer together, we're still family-Did I mention that her uncle happens to be Jay Hitt?

I would also like to express my gratitude to my grandparents, Hollis Child, Gloria Julian Child, and Paul Kalal. You believed in me when sometimes I didn't believe in myself. And thank you to my aunts and uncle, Gloria Ann Child, Paul Kalal, Jr. (my godfather) and Gerry Kalal. You've proven that family is family no matter how near, how far or how often we see each other.

Thank you to the rest of my extended family-the Perrys, the O'Neills, the Kalals, etc. We've been together for weddings and funerals, babies and reunions. Watching you celebrate God during the happy times and find comfort through God during the hard times has made my faith grow stronger. And no one can party like my family.

I've had many friends over the years that have made a difference in my life. Originally I had planned to thank each and every one of you, but we decided that it was inappropriate for the acknowledgements to be longer than the book. If you'd like to read the full acknowledgements check it out at tracylovesray.com

To all of my friends past, future and present I'd like to offer this quote- "Some people come into our lives and quickly go. Some stay for awhile and leave footprints on our hearts and we are never, ever the same." Anonymous

There have also been many people who have influenced my life that are no longer with us. They are June Child, Sally Kalal, Mike Smith, Matthew Wiseman, Beth Andrews, Staff Sergeant Joseph Goodrich, Anthony Guercio, Diane Leeson, and DaNiyah Jackson.

I offer this quote in their memory-"And I know you're shining down on me from heaven, Like so many friends we lost along the way, And I know eventually we'll be together, One sweet day."-Mariah Carey and Boys II Men.

I'd like to thank Brett Mason for doing the cover art and Lorna Lynch for being our editor. And of course, a million thank yous to Jay Hitt for noticing a few simple words on an overpass in Ohio.

FOREWARD

A few years ago, I was driving through Ohio and I happened to look up at an overpass and noticed the graffiti written on it. It said "Tracy Loves Ray". It was bold and written in very bright colors and I know that when something is written in bold letters and very bright colors, it must be true. And I wondered about the person who'd written on the overpass. Who would go to such lengths to make this declaration of love and devotion? Having no answer, I made one up and wrote the song, "Tracy Loves Ray". Now Theresa Child has taken Tracy and Ray and a host of characters and provided the answer I was looking for. I know you'll enjoy this story and I'm proud to have played a part in its creation. Thanks, Theresa.

Jay Hitt
July 2008

PRELUDE

There's something about a small town. Somehow the air seems cleaner, the people seem friendlier, and there's time to stop and smell the roses. Or tell a story.

Small-town living is taking a Sunday drive or sitting on the front porch sipping a glass of lemonade or maybe an ice-cold beer. A traffic jam is two cars stopped at an intersection. Doors can be left unlocked after dark. Families eat home-cooked meals together.

Everybody knows everybody and everybody's business. Kids grow up together and remain friends until they die. People marry their high-school sweethearts and stay married until they die.

That's how it is in Chardon, Ohio. There's a group of guys who have known each other since birth that meet for brunch at Jimmy's Diner every Saturday morning. They've been doing it for about thirty years. They meet at 11:00 a.m. on the dot and order steak and eggs, blueberry pancakes, and Belgian waffles with all the trimmings — bacon, sausage, hash browns, and home fries. And they tell stories. True stories about their lives and their families' lives. And some not-so-true stories of fishing trips and girls they dated in high school.

I like to spend Saturday afternoons at Jimmy's Diner listening to the men tell their stories. I get a kick out of watching the guys interrupt and correct each other. I also enjoy how Rebecca, who owns the diner, adds a woman's point of view to the mix. I never know what to expect from the tales. I've laughed until my belly hurts; I've cried so many times I started stashing Kleenex in my pocket; and on occasion, I've found myself looking at the world in a new way. One story makes me do all three, my favorite story: "Tracy Loves Ray." A love story.

Now, I've heard the story of "Tracy Loves Ray" more than once and I could hear it over and over again. But I will never forget the first time Finny's granddaughter Tracy heard the tale. These days eight-year-old Tracy is a fixture at the Saturday gab sessions, but at the time she was still pretty new to the tradition. Already, Tracy had fallen madly in love with the stories her grandpa and friends told. She'd listen intently and ask all kinds of questions and beg to hear "at least one more before we go, Grandpa!"

On this particular fall day when it came time to tell stories, the leader, Sunny, announced that Tracy had made a request for a story. Tracy was an animated child by nature, but that day she was exceptionally excited. She had just seen the overpass that had been painted with the words, "Tracy Loves Ray," and wanted to know the whole story. Tracy always wanted to know the WHOLE story. And the folks at Jimmy's Diner were happy to tell her. So here it is, the story of a curious little girl visiting her grandfather, and the story of "Tracy Loves Ray" told to her by the townspeople who lived it.

Chapter 1

It was almost time for Tracy's surprise, and Finny could barely contain his excitement.

Finny Coleman and his eight-year-old granddaughter were on their way to Jimmy's Diner for brunch and stories with his friends from the "Chardon Volleyballers." But they had a stop to make first.

From the time Tracy was a baby, Finny had enjoyed helping her explore the world. He found that the more he showed her the more she wanted to see. That's why he couldn't wait for this surprise. As far as he was concerned it was long overdue. He only wished his wife could be there to experience it with them. She would have loved sharing with her granddaughter all the special memories that their family had created there. "In fact," he thought, "that's probably why I haven't brought Tracy sooner." Her grandmother had been too weak to leave the house for the last few years of her life, and after she died it was too hard for Finny to go there. "Now is the right time," he decided, "and I believe there is an angel in heaven watching over us today as Tracy visits the place that is the root of her family."

Finny smiled as he made the right hand turn. "Okay, Tracy, see the house on the right? This is the house where Grandma and I raised our family, the place where your mother and Uncle Shawn grew up. We affectionately referred to it as 'Coleman Castle.'" Finny had pulled the car in front of a three-story sky-blue Victorian. As they got out, he pointed out the wrap-around porch that Grandma had loved, and his favorite feature, the large bay window on the bottom floor. Tracy thought they were nice, but was more impressed with the large yard.

"When your mother was your age she used to swing on that swing and climb that tree. And over there is the tree house your uncle Shawn and I built when he was ten."

"This house is so cool. Why did you and Grandma move?" Tracy asked.

"It did make us sad to leave," he admitted, "but in a lot of ways it would have made us more sad to stay. We were dealing with what people call 'empty nest syndrome.'"

"What's that, Grandpa?"

"Empty nest syndrome basically means that we were lonely. You see, we had sold our sports store, your mom had just married your dad, and your uncle Shawn was in college in California.

"The house was so empty with just the two of us that Grandma and I decided it was time to see the world — or at the very least, the United States. Our goal was to visit each of the fifty states. And we did. We went to the capitol and saw the White House. We visited Mount Rushmore, rode the rapids of the Colorado River in the Grand Canyon, and gambled in Vegas."

"What was your favorite state?" asked Tracy.

"I'm not sure if I would say it was our favorite, but we spent almost six months in California. Your Grandma always loved the Pacific Ocean and we could be near Shawn."

"Do you love the Pacific Ocean, too, Grandpa?"

"Well, I wasn't always a beach person. My family never went to the beach when I was growing up. The first time I saw an ocean was when we took your mother and Shawn to Ocean City, Maryland. We had such a great time that the next year we invited all your grandma's brothers and sisters and their families to join us. We rented a huge house and I played golf with the men while your grandmother and the ladies worked on their tans and watched the kids playing on the beach. It became a tradition for the whole family to vacation in Ocean City during the last two weeks in July. So, yes, I do love the ocean. Whether it's the Pacific or the Atlantic Ocean I love smelling salt in the air, taking a nap on the sand, and feasting on fresh seafood . . ."

"If you love the ocean so much, why did you come back here?" Tracy interrupted.

"You ask the most insightful questions, Tracy. And I have a good answer for you. Uncle Shawn was graduating and moving back here, and your mom was pregnant with you. Grandma and I couldn't bear the thought of missing a single moment with our family. Sure, sometimes we missed sunny California, but one smile from you would brighten our day so much that Ohio was the sunniest place on earth. I guess the real answer is love. Love for you, for your mom and dad, for Shawn, for our friends, and for this little town in Ohio that we've called home all of our lives. Love, Tracy, love is the answer."

Finny realized that he had gone a bit overboard. It was easy for him to get carried away on the subject of love and family. From the moment Tracy was born, both he and his wife prayed that Tracy would experience the same love that they had been surrounded with in their lives.

Finny wasn't sure what to say next.

"Hey, that's Tanner, Zack, and Courtney!" Tracy exclaimed as three children emerged from the house.

"Grandma and I were pleased when Miss Becca and Matt decided to buy this house for Susan and Jeff to raise their family," Grandpa said. Rebecca and Matt were old friends of Finny's and owners of Jimmy's Diner. "Let's go say hi."

Tracy ran towards her friends. "Tanner! Zack! Courtney! I'm so happy to see you. Can I swing on your swing? I want to swing just like my mom did when she was a kid."

"We've been waiting for you to get here," said Courtney. "Gramps said we can play with you until Dad comes home."

Finny turned to address Matt, the older gentleman who had followed the children out the door. "Thanks for letting us stop by. I think showing Tracy the home where her mom grew up will help to ease some of the sadness of the last year."

"Yes, it has been hard for you," Matt agreed. "But you're definitely at your best when you're with that little girl. I'm sure you've been having fun babysitting while Gloria and Hollis are at their medical convention. When do they get back?"

"Tracy and I are picking them up at the airport after brunch. Hard to believe the week is already over."

Finny and Matt sat on the porch in rocking chairs and drank coffee while the kids played. The two had become fast friends when Matt moved to Chardon almost forty years earlier. They shared a love for small-town living and family life. They didn't look anything alike, however. Matt towered over Finny at six foot four compared to Finny's five foot ten. Matt's blond hair and blue eyes complimented his tan. Other than a slight beer belly, he was lean and trim. Finny had brown eyes and brown hair peppered with gray, but he also kept fit.

As Finny rocked in his chair, he couldn't keep his eyes off his blue-eyed, blond-haired granddaughter who was grinning ear to ear while Tanner pushed her on the swing.

About fifteen minutes later, Jeff pulled into the driveway. Matt left for the diner while Finny and Jeff chatted about some of the changes Jeff and Susan had made to the house. Finny approved of most of the changes, although he wasn't a big fan of the pink flamingos Susan had used to decorate the yard.

It wasn't long before Finny told Tracy it was time leave Coleman Castle and head for the diner. Tracy didn't want to leave the other children until he reminded her that she would see them at church the next day.

On the way to the diner, Tracy asked a million questions.

"What's that guy doing?"

"Trimming the bushes."

"What kind of dog is that?"

"German Shepherd."

"How many leaves do you think are on that tree?"

"Eight thousand, five hundred and thirty-seven."

As Finny tried to quench her thirst for knowledge he barely noticed the beautiful day or that they had reached the overpass on Turner Road.

"Grandpa, wait! Stop the car!"

Finny slammed on the brakes and looked to see what had startled Tracy.

She turned around and pointed at the overpass. "I just saw my name on the outside of that tunnel! Can we go back and read what it says?"

Finny took a deep breath and said, "Tracy, try not to yell so loud when I'm driving. You scared me. I thought you were hurt or I was going to run over an animal."

Still, he backed the car slowly through the overpass keeping an eye out for any other cars that might be coming down the road.

After safely making it through the concrete tunnel, he pulled over and waited patiently for Tracy to speak.

The overpass had become part of the folklore of Chardon, but it certainly wasn't because of its appearance. It was just a small tunnel, crumbling in spots, and there were overgrown bushes along the sides and a railing across the top that hid the train tracks on which trains traveled once or twice a day. The overpass had become legendary because of the words painted in red.

"It says 'Tracy Loves Ray,'" Tracy told her grandfather. "It's pretty faded, but I can still read it. How do you think it got there, Grandpa?"

Finny paused, deciding how much of the story to tell Tracy.

"Well, the first time "Tracy Loves Ray" appeared on the overpass was in 1970. As the story goes, Tracy wanted Ray to have a note for him to see every day so that he would never forget how much she loved him."

"But, Grandpa, 1970 was a long time ago. How can 'Tracy Loves Ray' still be written on the wall?"

"Each year for their anniversary Tracy repainted the overpass so that Ray would never, ever forget that she loved him."

"It looks like it's about time for Tracy to repaint it."

Finny looked at the faded message for a moment. "Yes, it certainly does. Now, how about we get on over to the diner and get us some breakfast?

Chapter 2

I wanted to tell you the story of "Tracy Loves Ray" for two reasons. First, it's a great story. Second, I want to dispel some of the myths about small-town folk. People from the city often consider us hicks or make jokes about inbreeding. Sometimes it's those of us who reside in small towns who complain the most about small-town living. Many times I have longed to live in a city where I could be anonymous. I've found that in Chardon if a person sneezes on one side of town, the next day the people on the other side are asking if their cold is getting better.

But overall, I am grateful to live in a small town. It's nice to know your neighbors and to know you can count on them when times are tough. The people in Chardon played such a major role in Tracy and Ray's story that I believe it shows the heart of small-town living, and that the core of who Tracy and Ray are can be found in their family relationships and friendships.

Technically, Chardon is a city. After the 2000 census the population went just above 5,000 and the village was automatically designated the City of Chardon. But other than a few political adjustments, such as the creation of voting wards, there are not many differences between Chardon the City and Chardon the Village.

The heart of the town is Chardon Square. Built in the first half of the nineteenth century, Chardon Square was to be the town common area. It consisted of a grassy area surrounded by the vital elements of small-town life, including schools, churches, the courthouse, and town hall.

Quaint, family-run shops have replaced most of the buildings along the perimeter of the square, although the Chardon Public Library is still there, along with several government offices, law offices, and the largest building in the square, the courthouse.

Set off by itself at the north end, the red brick courthouse is the highlight of the square. The oversized windows and the tower with its four clocks telling the time north, south, east, and west make it an impressive structure.

The grassy area is home to several historic artifacts, including Chardon's first fire bell. At the edge closest to the courthouse is a replica of the bandstand originally built in the square in 1875.

Many events and activities take place in Chardon Square every year, including the annual Maple Festival which began in 1926. After these events many people head one block north to Jimmy's Diner to grab a burger and fries before going home for the night.

You may think it's odd, but I've always had an affinity for diners; and I'm not alone. But I often wonder why people, myself included, go out of their way to cram into tight booths or to sit at a counter. What do we find appealing about gaudy linoleum floors, Formica countertops, and stainless steel? Sure, you always get a good meal, but it's never anything distinctive. It's your typical burger, meatloaf, and hot-turkey-sandwich fare.

I think what I like about a diner is that I'm comfortable just being myself. Diners are without pretense; what you see is what you get. It's the simplicity I crave, a good meal and good conversation. No more, no less.

Jimmy's Diner is a classic railroad-car-style diner made of stainless steel with red trim. Inside, the white linoleum floor has a red diamond design. The booths and stools are covered with red vinyl with white accents. The entrance is through a door at the end of the car. When you walk in there are booths along the length of the left side. The booths are usually taken by families enjoying a meal together or high school kids grabbing a burger and fries. I prefer to sit at the counter on the opposite side of the diner. I long to be a kid again and spin around and around on the stools. Behind the counter are the grill and a doorway that leads back to the prep area and bakery that Matt added on when he bought the place. At the far end of the car next to the counter are two more booths. Those booths and the two across from them are the ones Rebecca reserves for the Chardon Volleyballers on Saturday mornings.

Which reminds me, we should get back to our story.

Chapter 3

Finny and Tracy arrived at the diner shortly after 11:00 a.m. Most of the stools at the counter and all the booths were occupied. The twosome joined Matt in one of the booths reserved for the Chardon Volleyballers. Finny ordered a cup of coffee for himself and a glass of orange juice for his granddaughter.

Tracy and her family ate at the diner several times a month, but this was only the third time she had come to a storytelling session. She was already becoming familiar with the routine. First, the men made their rounds exchanging hugs and handshakes. Then they ate breakfast. When everyone finished eating, Sunny would stand up and ask if anyone had a story to share.

Even though the men had been telling stories for over thirty years, they never ran out of tales to tell. They spoke of growing up together, teachers they had at Chardon High School, and playing volleyball.

As teens, the guys spent much of their time together on the volleyball court. Soon, their girlfriends joined them and the games became a weekly ritual. The tradition almost ended during their college years when they could only play during breaks and summer vacations. But after graduation, the weekly games resumed and the friends began taking turns hosting get-togethers afterwards that would last until 1:00 a.m.

The Chardon Volleyballers were a close knit group. Each member had a nickname, many of them earned in childhood. They served as groomsmen and bridesmaids in each other's weddings and as godparents to each other's kids.

They spent Fourth of Julys, Memorial Days, and Labor Days together in Chardon Park grilling hamburgers and hot dogs, and munching on the salads and desserts the ladies made. They played volleyball and softball and threw horseshoes during the day and had spirited games of Trivial Pursuit and other board games by the fire at night.

At some point, the guys decided to get together on Saturday mornings to play golf. After they played eighteen holes, they headed to Jimmy's for brunch.

Over the years as the Volleyballers grew older and their lives grew busier, the volleyball games decreased from once a week to a game or two at holiday picnics. And the guys don't play golf more than a few times a year, but the brunch tradition lives on.

It would be a few minutes before her blueberry pancakes would be ready, so Tracy went up to the counter in search of Miss Becca to tell her about the visit to Coleman Castle. Miss Becca was one of Tracy's favorite people. When her grandmother was sick Tracy could ask her questions that she couldn't ask anyone else. Miss Becca was the one who explained to her what cancer was and that you couldn't catch it.

Tracy loved going to the diner because Miss Becca let her go back in the kitchen and watch the bakers make pies and the cooks put potatoes in the cutter for fresh cut French fries. And she gave Tracy fresh baked chocolate chip cookies.

Miss Becca came out of the kitchen. "It's about time you got here. I was just taking some cookies out of the oven. I know it's against the rules before breakfast, but let's sneak one for you while they're still warm. Come on back to the kitchen."

Finny watched them walk into the kitchen and smiled. He was no fool, he knew about the warm cookies. He figured it was harmless. In fact, it's something his wife would have done.

"So, Tracy, have you had a fun week with Grandpa?" Miss Becca asked.

"I sure have. Mom says it's good for Grandpa to have me around to keep him company." Tracy knew that Grandpa needed company because he was still sad about Grandma dying last year.

Grandma had been sick for a long time before she died. Almost for as long as Tracy could remember. But being sick didn't stop Grandma from doing all the important Grandma things. Tracy would crawl into bed with her and she would read Tracy's favorite books. She used funny voices and never told Tracy to pick a shorter book like her dad did. Tracy wished Grandma hadn't been so sick and could still read to her and give her hugs and kisses. And she knew Grandpa wished the same thing. So, Tracy was happy to be spending the week with Grandpa and be his company.

"Your grandfather loves spending this extra time with you," said Miss Becca. "And the other guys like it, too. In fact, they're hoping you'll start coming to Volleyballer story time every week."

"That would be awesome. Last time they told me how everybody got their nicknames."

"And how many do you remember?"

"I remember them all," Tracy said proudly and began to rattle off the stories one by one. "Uncle Sunny's real name is Raymond, but when he was little his mom called him her Ray of Sunshine, and all the kids in Sunday school made fun of him and called him Sunny. Kid is called Kid because he's Sunny's kid brother. Dodger got his name because he wasn't very good at dodging the ball when they played dodge ball. And they call Matt Brownie because he's a Cleveland Browns fan."

Tracy and Miss Becca walked out to the eating area and looked around the room to see who hadn't been mentioned yet. "What about Turtle?" Miss Becca asked.

"Turtle always moves slow like a turtle except on the volleyball court." Tracy saw two other Volleyballers she missed. "Trickster was always playing practical jokes on the other kids. And Newbie didn't join the group until way after everybody else, so that's where he got his name."

Miss Becca gave Tracy a high five and said, "You really did remember them all, Tracy. But what about your grandfather?"

"Grandpa's story is the best story of all. It was a long time ago when Grandpa was a teenager. It was summertime and he and his friends were volunteering at church camp . . .

༺༻

"Come on, Mr. Coleman. We have to finish with latrine duty so we can get back in time for swimming," said Trickster.

"I'm working as fast as I can, Mr. Benedict."

The twelve-year-old boys were having a good time at church camp, even if they did have to clean toilets and call each other by their surnames. Pastor Perry could be strict, but mostly he was an okay guy. He played volleyball with the guys, snuck them an extra treat at snack time, and didn't seem to mind too much when the boys played tricks on him.

Trickster rinsed out his sponge and said, "I think we're done. Let's take this stuff back to Pastor Perry's office and go jump in the lake."

Pastor Perry's office was what one would expect a minister's office to look like. It had shelves full of books and a desk covered with notes for his Sunday sermons. But what made his office unique was his collection of dolphin paraphernalia.

As a child Pastor Perry had dreamed of becoming a dolphin trainer. Often the pastor would include dolphin stories in his sermons. It became traditional for church members to give him dolphin memorabilia, and soon his office was filled with stuffed dolphins, dolphin knickknacks, and books about dolphins. On the easy chair in the corner lay a dolphin quilt made by one of the church ladies. On the desk was Pastor Perry's favorite dolphin, a small stuffed animal he affectionately called Finny.

"This place is crazy with dolphins," said Trickster as he put the cleaning supplies in the pastor's closet.

"Yeah, man. We could probably throw half of these dolphins away and he'd never notice."

"Well, he'd definitely miss Finny," commented Trickster as he threw the stuffed animal towards the other boy.

"Can you imagine the look on his face if his favorite dolphin disappeared?"

"That'd be a great trick."

The boys grinned at each other as they imagined Pastor Perry walking into his office and discovering Finny was gone.

Trickster grabbed the dolphin and put him back on the desk. "We'd better forget about pulling any pranks. My parents said that if I mess up during camp this summer I can't play soccer this year. Come on, Mr. Coleman, let's get out of here."

A few weeks later at the Sunday service Pastor Perry announced that Finny was missing. "I thought that I had misplaced him," he explained to the congregation, "but yesterday I received a package from Philadelphia. Inside there was a picture of Finny at the Liberty Bell and this letter."

He began reading. "Dear Pastor Perry: You talk a lot about destiny and God's plan. I've often wondered what God's plan is for me. I don't think I can find my destiny in your office, so I'm off to see the United States. Try not to worry about me. I've been a good dolphin and have attended church every Sunday. Your friend, Finny"

Soon the church was abuzz about the missing dolphin. Every time Pastor Perry got another letter it was printed in the church bulletin. Everyone wondered where Finny would go next. Washington, D.C.? Niagara Falls? Perhaps Disneyland?

The Sunday after Thanksgiving Pastor Perry began his sermon with a question. "What are you thankful for?"

"My kids."

"My home."

"God's love."

When the answers subsided Pastor Perry said, "I am grateful for many things. I have enough to eat, the love of my family, and good friends, many of whom are members of this congregation. But I feel especially blessed because when I went into my office Friday morning I discovered Finny sitting on my desk along with a note saying that he had seen all kinds of cool places and all kinds of neat things, but had discovered that he belonged in Chardon.

"I got to thinking. How did Finny travel around the country? As I looked over the letters and postcards I received from my dolphin friend it occurred to me that Finny was at Graceland at the same time as the O'Neills. I called Paul and he admitted to me that Finny had accompanied them on vacation per the request of one of the young men from the church. When they came home they gave Finny back to this person so he could be sent on another adventure.

"When Finny first disappeared, I was furious that someone would walk into my office and take him. Then I received the first package from Philadelphia. I was still annoyed, but also intrigued by this idea of Finny searching for his destiny. I found myself wondering about God's plan for me. I began looking for new ways to spread God's word and to do God's work. And then Finny came home. He had learned that his destiny was here. To me that speaks volumes. You don't always have to go searching for your calling. Perhaps God is calling us right now, but are we listening? I realized that we could all learn from Finny's journey. The fact that a teen-aged boy's prank turned into an important lesson proves to me that God does indeed work in mysterious ways, and for that I am thankful.

"I would like to introduce the young man who took us on this journey with Finny. Mr. Coleman, would you please come up here?"

Pastor Perry smiled at the young man standing sheepishly before him. "Mr. Coleman, what started as a trick has turned into a treat and in many ways a blessing. I have a feeling this is a story we'll be talking about for years to come. Therefore, I dub thee Finny. May you find your destiny just as Finny the dolphin did."

༺✦༻

"I will never forget that day," said Miss Becca. "I've never seen a face as red as your grandfather's when Pastor Perry nicknamed him Finny."

She headed back to the kitchen to take another batch of cookies out of the oven. When she saw that Tracy had followed her she asked, "So what did you think about seeing where your mother grew up?"

"I loved it," Tracy answered. "It's a real pretty house and I had a lot of fun on the swing. I bet Tanner, Zack, and Courtney really like living there."

"They sure do," Miss Becca agreed.

"Grandpa said he'd take me back some time so I can play with them. Maybe we can take them to see where it says 'Tracy Loves Ray' on the tunnel."

"When a railroad has a bridge going over a road it's called an overpass," Miss Becca said. "I didn't know your grandfather took you to see the overpass."

"He didn't really take me to see it, we just went by it on the way here. I noticed my name painted on the wall, so I asked Grandpa to back up so I could read the whole thing. Grandpa said that Tracy painted it so that Ray would be reminded every day that she loved him. I wonder why she couldn't just tell him or write him a note."

"Well, that's a long story."

"Maybe that could be one of the stories today."

Miss Becca transferred the cookies onto a cooling rack and took the hot cookie sheet to the sink. "I'm not sure that's such a good idea. It could upset Sunny. He's had a hard year losing his wife and sister within months of each other. It might make him sad to talk about Tracy."

"I don't want Uncle Sunny to feel sad. I can hear the story some other time."

"Well, let's wait and see. I'll talk it over with the guys. For now, Miss Tracy, I saw Sharon take your breakfast out a few minutes ago. You'd better go eat before it gets cold."

Tracy joined Finny and Matt at the table. Her grandfather was almost finished with his omelet and home fries. When he was done eating he got up and traveled the room talking to the other men. When he went over to talk to Sunny, Miss Becca joined them. Tracy wondered if they were talking about telling the Tracy Loves Ray story. When she saw Sunny turn away with tears in his eyes she knew it was unlikely she'd get to hear the story today.

A few minutes later, Finny walked back to the table and Sunny called the group to order. "Well, gang, it looks like we already have a request for a story. Tracy, would you like to tell us what you saw today?"

Tracy got over her surprise quickly. She stood up proudly and told the group about going to Coleman Castle and swinging on the swing. She told them about driving to the diner and seeing the Tracy Loves Ray overpass. "What I was wondering is why Tracy didn't just tell Ray every day that she loved him or put notes in his lunchbox like my mom does."

Sunny cleared his throat. "That's an excellent question. Who would like to begin the story?"

Miss Becca spoke up. "I'll begin. After all, I was working the day Tracy told Ray about her job offer in California." Miss Becca saw little Tracy sitting next to her grandfather and thought she should give a little background.

"The story begins before Matt and I owned the diner — actually, before we had even met. It was the spring after Tracy and Ray had graduated from college.

"Tracy was a pretty girl with blond hair and blue eyes. Everyone loved her, she was so perky and full of life. She was funny and never had a mean word to say about anyone. She was my best friend.

"I remember back when we were in high school. Tracy kept me company when it was my turn to work at the diner during the football game. I'd only get one or two customers because everybody in town was at the stadium rooting for the Hilltoppers. Tracy loved football, so it meant a lot that she would skip the game to hang out with me. We drank coffee and talked for hours.

"We talked about her relationship with Ray and the steady stream of losers that I dated. We talked about our hopes, and our fears, and our dreams. We both dreamt of getting out of this town. We wanted to live in a big city where people didn't stick their nose into other people's business and where there was something fun to do.

"The only thing that held her back was her love for Ray. And who could blame her? Even I had a crush on Ray. He wasn't movie-star handsome, but there was just something about him. It may have even been his devotion to Tracy that I found so attractive. He was such a cutie with his dark hair and dreamy brown eyes. He played a lot of sports, so he could eat anything on the diner menu without gaining a pound.

"Ray and Tracy made a great couple; they even looked like they belonged together. And they only had eyes for each other. They spent so much time together no one thought they would survive being apart. . . ."

Chapter 4

Tracy arrived at the diner to meet Ray for dinner promptly at 6:30 p.m. Business was booming and she discovered that their usual booth was already occupied. Becca gestured that one of the corner booths was free.

"Hey, Tracy. Would you like a glass of tea or is it a milkshake kind of day?"

"I'm actually thinking about a root beer float."

Becca knew something was up. Tracy only ordered floats when she was nervous. Root beer floats and cheese fries were how Tracy made it through finals during her college years.

"Is everything okay? The last time you ordered a float was when Ray asked you to move in with him. You've been living together at least six months now. Did you have a fight or do you just have a big job interview coming up?" Tracy had just graduated from Cooper University, a small school a couple of towns away, and was looking for a job in the field of graphic design. She was hoping to find something in Cleveland so she could explore city life.

Tracy hesitated. "Something like that. . . ."

In an attempt to change the subject Tracy pointed to the "For Sale" sign hanging in the window and asked, "Don't you think it's about time Jimmy gives up trying to sell the diner?"

"Yeah, Jimmy's got about as much of a chance of leaving this town as I do. You're so lucky you got to go to school. You really have a shot of getting out of this place. Not me, I'll be a grandmother and still slinging coffee in this diner."

Tracy didn't answer, so Becca went behind the counter, turned in an order of cheese fries to the cook, and began to make the root beer float.

The door opened and Ray rushed in. "What a great day. Now that spring is here we'll be able to play volleyball outside," he said as he joined Tracy in the booth.

Becca brought over Tracy's drink and a cup of coffee for Ray. He saw the float and said, "Looks like our girl had a rough day. I hope you already put in an order for cheese fries."

"Before I made the float. They should be up soon."

Tracy and Ray gave Becca the rest of their order and she hurried off to take care of her other customers.

"So, my dear, would you like to tell me about your day now or do you want your fries first?"

"I'm not sure where to begin."

"Tell me about your big interview. I'm guessing it wasn't the good news you were hoping for."

"Oh, Ray. It was more than I could hope for. It's a great job. I must have really impressed them because they usually don't give someone fresh out of school a position like this. And everybody was so friendly. I can just tell this is the company I'm meant to be working for."

"That's wonderful, honey. What's with the float and the fries then?"

"There is one drawback to this job," Tracy admitted slowly. "I would have to move to LA."

"LA?"

"Yeah, you know Los Angles, the city of angels."

"What are you talking about? The job you interviewed for is in Cleveland."

Becca walked over to the table, discreetly set down the basket of cheese fries, and walked away.

Tracy picked up a fry and twirled it between her fingers. "Yes. But that position was already filled. It turns out they opened a new office in LA a few months ago and they're still in the process of hiring. They think I'd be perfect for their new division."

"I see. So, this is the first job offer you get, and you just take it?"

"I didn't take it, Ray. Not yet anyway. I told them I had to think about it, and that I wanted to talk it over with you."

Ray remained silent so Tracy continued. "The thing is, this is a dream come true for me. It's a great job and to live in LA would be exciting. It would be a chance to see new things, meet new people, and to go to the beach every day. I had so much fun last year when the girls and I went to Florida for spring break. Imagine the adventures you and I could have in California."

Ray saw how much the job meant to her. "Okay, okay. Let's think about this rationally. On the one hand, a move across the country would be taking a huge leap of faith. We know you have a job, but what am I going to do for work? On the other hand, I haven't had much luck finding a teaching position here and they probably need lots of teachers in California. When would we have to go?"

"I'd have to be there next week."

"Well, that settles it. That's just not enough time. We have an apartment to pack and arrangements to make. Even though it is just a maintenance job, I should still give the school district two week's notice. And how can we find somewhere decent to live in LA on such short notice?"

"The company will give me a furnished apartment that I can use until we find something else. All I would really need are clothes."

Tracy waited for Ray to say something. When he remained silent, she said, "It's okay, Ray. It was a dumb idea. I'm sure I can find an even better job in Cleveland."

"No, wait," Ray said reluctantly as he took her hands in his. "Maybe this could work. I knew it was just a matter of time until we made the move to Cleveland. Moving to LA is a big step, but when it comes down to it, it's not *that* different from moving to Cleveland."

"What are you saying?"

"I'm saying you should take the job. You could go to LA now and I'll stay back until you settle in. I'll pack up the apartment and join you then."

"Oh, Ray. How did I ever get so lucky? I'll write you every day and call you all the time and then you'll be there. It'll be like we were never apart."

"Somehow I doubt that, but we'll get through it. It'll be worth it when we're together again. Let's work out the details later. For now why don't you tell me about the job?"

Before she could answer Becca returned with the rest of their order and a coffee refill for Ray. The couple filled their friend in on the new development.

"This is cause for celebration. How about we get the gang together for a going away dinner on Sunday night?" Becca suggested.

Ray didn't want to share Tracy with anyone else during their precious little time left, but he knew the gang would want to say goodbye to her, too. "Sunday works for me. How about you, Tracy?"

As Tracy nodded in agreement it hit her that she would be moving to California in a week. She was going to leave her family and friends and the only life she had known. "Um, Becca, do you think I could get another root beer float?"

Chapter 5

Tracy was frantically looking for her lucky boots. She couldn't go to LA without them. Becca and their friend Stacey had dropped by the apartment with a bottle of wine to help her pack and they were almost finished. They had packed everything with the exception of toiletries and those darn boots.

Tracy sat on the edge of the bed and began to cry.

"I don't see why you're so upset about those boots," Stacey said as she threw her arms around Tracy. "You've had them since high school and the heel is falling off the left one."

"Maybe it's a sign. Maybe it means I shouldn't go. How can I leave you guys? How can I leave Ray?"

Becca knelt in front of Tracy. "The three of us have been best friends for fifteen years. I can't imagine a shopping trip or gossip session without you. But I love you and I want you to be happy. This is an amazing opportunity. You can't pass it up."

"How can I leave everything I know and everyone I love behind?"

Stacey answered, "We'll write and call and in a year or two we should be able to save enough to come visit you. I've always wanted to see California."

Tracy was beginning to calm down. "But what about Ray? We've decided to wait at least a month or two and see how the job works out before we even pick a date for him to come to California. Distance never did a lover good and time does things you never thought it would. He could forget all about me or find somebody else."

"There is no one else for Ray. The two of you are meant for each other," said Stacey.

"But I see the way the other girls look at him. Even Becca has a crush on him."

Becca bowed her head in agreement. "But he loves you."

"And I love him. I just need to remind him how much I love him, like the notes my mom used to leave in my lunchbox when I was a kid. I want to leave Ray a note he can see every day."

"I thought you were planning on writing to him every day. Don't you think that's enough?" asked Rebecca.

"No, I need something more. A sign of our love." She was quiet for a moment. "That's it, I know what to do! Will you help me, girls?"

Tracy began filling in her friends on her plan when Ray walked in. In his right hand was the missing pair of boots.

"Ray, what are you doing with my boots?"

"Well, I know they're your lucky boots, so I got new heels put on for you."

Stacey laughed and said, "How's that for a sign?"

༺ඏ༻

It was late Saturday afternoon. Tracy, Becca, and Stacey were at the overpass on Turner Road. They didn't have much time. It was difficult to convince Ray to let Tracy out of his sight and his arms for more than an hour or two. In addition, the couple was celebrating her new job with her parents and two brothers later that evening at the diner.

The sun warmed their backs as Rebecca and Stacey watched Tracy paint. The girls had offered to help, but Tracy wanted to do it herself. She wanted this message to be from her for Ray.

The work itself was easy, but time consuming. A couple cans of spray paint were the only tools she needed. She had borrowed a ladder from Trickster, but it turned out it was easier to squeeze through the railing on top of the overpass and paint upside down.

"There. I think it's done."

Becca and Stacey stepped back and surveyed Tracy's work. In great big red letters, Tracy had painted the words "TRACY LOVES RAY," although instead of a "V" Tracy had drawn a heart.

Tracy climbed down the hill to join her friends and check her graffiti. "It's a little sappy," she said, "but I'm a little sappy, too."

"It's perfect."

"It's beautiful."

"Ray'll love it."

Tracy shook her head. "No, there's something missing. Little hearts maybe. Or X's and O's."

"No, Trace. That would make it too sappy. Leave it like it is," Becca insisted.

Tracy racked her brain for that extra something that would complete her declaration of love, but came up with nothing.

Chapter 6

Tracy and Ray were in his Volkswagen Beetle headed for the last group dinner before she left for LA. Tracy was getting antsy. For what felt like the hundredth time, she began doubting her decision. *I'll never survive without the support of Becca and Stacey and I'll be lonely without my family and friends. But Ray will be joining me soon and I'll make new friends. And I'll be so busy setting up the apartment and starting a new job, I won't have time to be lonely.*

What if I can't find a grocery store or a place to get my hair done?

But it will be fun to explore a new city and escape the boredom of living in Chardon.

I may not like the job. Or maybe I won't be good at it.

But how can I let such a great opportunity pass me by?

And her worst fear. *What if the sophisticated people of LA don't want anything to do with some fuddy-duddy from Chardon, Ohio?*

Tracy silenced the voices in her head and reminded herself to focus on the evening of fun that lay ahead. She held her breath when Ray made the turn onto Turner Road.

Ray stopped the car when he saw their friends standing on the side of the road. "What is this?" he asked.

He saw the words painted on the overpass and tears welled up in his eyes. Barely able to speak, he took Tracy's hands, looked into her eyes, and whispered, "And Ray loves Tracy."

For several minutes, Ray and Tracy held each other. After an elongated kiss, they emerged from the car. Their friends surrounded them and there was much hugging, kissing, and crying.

Becca and Stacey had set up a picnic dinner so that the group could enjoy the beautiful spring evening. Sitting on blankets in the field by the overpass, they munched on fried chicken, potato salad, and strawberry shortcake.

"Do you think we could steal Tracy away from you for a minute? Stacey and I have something special we want to give her," Becca said to Ray.

"Not for too long I hope."

While Tracy was busy with her two best friends, Ray walked over to Dodger and said, "I have an idea. Do you happen to have any paint in the truck?" Dodger was famous for always having whatever you happened to need in his truck.

Dodger nodded, walked to the truck, and pulled out a can of black spray paint.

Ray took the paint from his friend. "I think Tracy's tied up with Stacey and Becca, but if you see her coming this way, could you distract her until I'm done?"

The twosome set off on their individual missions. Ray finished long before Tracy was done with her girlfriends. Other members of the group noticed what he had painted and gathered in front of the overpass to see when Tracy would notice.

Finally, Tracy walked over to the overpass. "What's going on over here?"

"Tracy, why did you spell my name wrong?" Ray asked.

"What? I didn't spell . . . Oh, Ray. This is why I love you. I knew there was something missing."

On the side of the overpass below and to the left of the words "TRACY LOVES RAY" was the additional declaration "AND HE LOVES HER TOO."

Tracy was amazed at how life can show you the correct path. At the beginning of the evening, she had been so worried she was making the wrong decision. She had feared that this final night with her friends would make her feel worse about her choice. But instead, the opposite had happened. The time with her friends reminded her that no matter how far apart they were, they had a bond that couldn't be broken.

Rebecca and Stacey's gift was the thing that clinched it for her. They had made her a beautiful photo album with pictures from all the years that they had been friends. They had even met secretly with her family to get pictures from them as well. Tracy knew that during any lonely times in LA she would be able to cure her homesickness by perusing the album. And if she got really down in the dumps, she could turn to the last page, which was the best surprise of all. Rebecca had arranged for Tracy's parents to drop by the overpass with their Polaroid camera and take a picture of the whole group in front of the colorful announcement, "TRACY LOVES RAY. AND HE LOVES HER TOO".

Chapter 7

True to her word, Tracy wrote to Ray every day.

March 28, 1975

Tracy Loves Ray
From Out on the West Coast
To Deep in Your Heart

My darling Ray,

I arrived in LA today around noon. One of the girls from my division, Michele, met me at the airport and took me to the new apartment. She's really sweet. She offered to pick me up for my first day of work tomorrow and show me around. She even wants to take me to lunch.

The apartment is small. There's only one bedroom, but the windows are huge and let in lots of sun. I think putting up some pictures and hanging some plants will make it feel more homey. Of course, it will never feel like home until you're here. . . .

April 5, 1975

Tracy Loves Ray
From Out on the West Coast
To Deep in Your Heart

Ray, my love,

What a great first week. Everyone at work is so nice. My boss wants me to work on a presentation for one of our biggest clients. Michele and I are going to work on it together. Today a bunch of us packed our lunches and walked to a park close to our building. I can't believe I was worried about making friends. It did make me kind of sad, though, because I couldn't help thinking the last time I had a picnic was at the overpass. . . .

April 25, 1975

Tracy Loves Ray
From Out on the West Coast
To Deep in Your Heart

Honeybunch,

    I talked to Becca today. I can't believe they sold the diner. It's been up for sale for two years and no one even looked at it. I'm gone for less than a month and it's sold! I bet Jimmy's thrilled. Now he can move to New Mexico and retire like he wanted.

    Becca said some bigwig from Cleveland bought the diner for his son, Matt something. Imagine being our age and owning your own restaurant. I think she's nervous about working for somebody new. She said she's thinking about looking for a job in Cleveland, anyway. I hope it all works out for her.

    It was so great to hear her voice. Exchanging letters isn't the same as talking on the phone or hanging out at the diner. Thank God you'll be here soon. Our once a week phone calls just aren't enough. . . .

May 19, 1975

Tracy Loves Ray
From Out on the West Coast
To Deep in Your Heart

Dearest Ray,

    Today was a strange day. Michele took me to an art gallery. I found a great painting of some children playing in the surf of the Pacific Ocean. When I was hanging it I accidentally put a hole in the wall and had to ask the super to fix it. He's quite a character. His name is Jay Hitt and he's a singer/songwriter. I've never heard of a singer being a superintendent before. I guess most singers in LA have day jobs. He invited me to go to one of his shows. Michele and I may do that next weekend.

    I'm so glad we've finally picked a date for you to come out here. I am counting the days until your arrival on July 13th (55 days). I never thought we'd be apart this long. I look at the picture of the gang in front of the overpass every night before I go to bed. Sometimes, I wonder if I'm ever looking at the picture at the same time you're looking at the overpass. . . .

July 20, 1975

Tracy Loves Ray
From Out on the West Coast
To Deep in Your Heart

My True Love,

    How is your mother? Please send her my love. I sent her a letter to let her know that one of the reasons I love you so much is your devotion to your family. I told her that even if you had come to LA when we planned, I would have sent you right back to take care of her. She can't be trying to cook and clean with a broken leg. She needs to stop feeling guilty and concentrate on getting better.
    On a lighter note, our big presentation went well. The client really enjoyed it. It's a good thing, too because apparently the company is counting on this project to keep us afloat. . . .

August 28, 1975

Tracy Loves Ray
From Out on the West Coast
To Deep in Your Heart

My Beloved Ray,

  I am so glad your mother is feeling better. It must be a relief to be out of that cast. Unfortunately, it looks like we'll have to put off our reunion for a bit longer. Ever since we lost our biggest client in the beginning of August, it's only been a matter of time and now it's official. The company I work for is closing down. They told me today, I'd better look around. . . .

Chapter 8

Tracy had discovered that if she spent her mornings submitting applications and going to interviews and the afternoons venturing through LA, it took some of the sting out of being unemployed. She had a line on a few jobs and was hopeful that she would be back on track before she had to be out of her apartment by the end of October.

Over the past two weeks since she had lost her job she had thought about giving up and going back to Ohio. Ray had been offered a job at the high school as a history teacher and coach of the volleyball team. The diner's new owner Matt had asked Becca out, and Stacey claimed he was a perfect match for her. Tracy was dying to meet him. There was so much going on at home and she was missing it.

But the more she explored LA, the more she grew to love California. She visited museums and art galleries. She and Michele had gone to see her landlord Jay Hitt perform several times. Most of all she loved the ocean and the weather there, the California savoir faire.

Today, Tracy had decided to spend the afternoon at the beach. It was a dry hot day. The water was refreshing as she played in the surf. She emerged from the water and fell asleep on her towel. She woke up several hours later to discover that it was sunset and most of the swimmers, surfers, and sunbathers had left and she was all but alone on the beach.

As she watched the sun go down over the ocean, she thought of Ray. What was he doing? Was he thinking of her, too?

෴෴෴

A few weeks later, Tracy was back at the beach for the afternoon. The day before, she had had a second interview at PAK, Inc., an up and coming company. Her previous bosses had given her a glowing recommendation and as luck would have it Michele's latest boyfriend was the manager of the editing department and had put in a good word for her.

Things were looking up.

Tracy was ready to enjoy a relaxing Saturday afternoon swimming and tanning. She was stretched out on her towel about to begin a new book when Tom, head of operations at her old job, appeared out of nowhere.

"Mind if I join you?" he asked.

"Of course not, it's good to see you."

He spread out his towel and plopped down in the sand. "So what have you been up to? Any luck finding a new job?"

"I have an interview with PAK, Inc. Ever heard of it?"

"Of course. It's an excellent company. Good pay and great benefits."

Tom took off his shirt and Tracy couldn't help but notice his well-tanned, muscular chest. "Keep your fingers crossed for me," she said.

"To be honest, I was hoping you hadn't found a job. There's a position opening in my division that I think you'd be perfect for. If it doesn't work out with PAK, promise me you'll give me a call."

She agreed to take him up on the offer. "How's Debbie?" she asked.

"We broke up not long after the company went under."

"I'm so sorry."

"Don't be. It was a long time coming. We didn't have much in common. I love the beach, she loves the pool. I'd rather be outside riding bikes or roller skating, she'd rather be inside reading a book."

"That sounds like me and Ray, but somehow it works for us."

They spent close to an hour chatting. The sun was hot that day, so in between stories they took dips in the ocean. Later they took a walk along the coast. By the time they got back to their towels, the sun was beginning to set. Tom asked Tracy to have dinner with him. "Just a burger and fries, there's a small diner not far from here."

"That sounds great. I haven't had this much fun in a while, I'm not ready to go home yet."

At the diner they ran into Michele and her boyfriend. The foursome ate together and went dancing afterwards. By the time Tracy got home, it was after midnight and she was exhausted. She fell into bed and fell asleep almost immediately. As she closed her eyes, she realized that she had forgotten to write to Ray.

Chapter 9

Tracy woke up the next morning, made a cup of coffee, and began a letter to Ray. The letter went on for four pages without saying much at all. She told him about going to the diner and how it made her homesick for Jimmy's. She devoted an entire page to the differences between the two diners making sure to point out that the LA diner had its charms as well. She described in great detail the club where she had gone dancing with her friends. She wrote about every little moment of the past few days, but even though she mentioned the interview that Tom wanted to set up for her, she never mentioned him by name. She had written about Tom in some of her earlier letters, but now it seemed different. She tried not to give it too much thought as she licked the stamp and hurried to the post office to send the letter on its way.

Tracy spent the rest of the day running errands and cleaning the apartment. Ray called around 7:30 p.m. They had only talked for about fifteen minutes before they got into a fight about when Ray should come to California.

Ray told Tracy, "Look, this is ridiculous. My mother's leg is healed, the landlord wants to know when he should start looking for a new tenant, and I've been living out of boxes for months."

"I know, Ray. But if I get the job with PAK, I'm going to have to move to San Francisco. No matter what I've got to be out of this apartment soon. Just wait another week or two and I'll get everything straightened out here."

"I'm tired of waiting. I don't care if we have to move as soon as I get there. I just want to be with you."

"I understand that. But don't you think that I have enough to deal with right now without having to deal with you, too?"

"So, now I'm just another thing you have to deal with?"

"That's not what I meant," Tracy whispered.

"I know. Look, obviously we're not getting anywhere tonight. How about I call you tomorrow and we'll talk about it some more."

"Okay."

"Tracy, I love you."

"I love you, too."

As she hung up the phone Tracy wasn't sure who had meant it less when they said "I love you," her or Ray.

༄༅༄༅

The next day Tracy received a phone call from Bob, the head of personnel at PAK, Inc. He informed her that the president of the company had hired his nephew to take the position that she had interviewed for. "I'm so disappointed," he told her. "You would be perfect for the job. If anything comes up, you'll be the first person I'll call."

She was touched by the sentiment, but realized that if she didn't get a job soon, she was going to have to go back home. She had to be out of the apartment in a week and she was running out of money.

Maybe I should go home. I miss Ray. I miss my family and the gang. Tracy began to cry softly. *But if I left it would be admitting defeat. And I love it here, too. It's a new world to explore. There are people here I care about. Michele and her boyfriend. Jay. And now Tom.*

That's when Tracy remembered Tom's job offer. She grabbed the phone and realized that the only phone number she had for Tom was his home number, and it was the middle of the afternoon. Tom would still be at work. So she went for a run in the park around the corner.

On her way back home she was pleasantly surprised to see Tom walking towards her. "Hey there. What are you doing here? Shouldn't you be at work?"

"I'm on my way back to the office. I have a meeting with my boss when I get back. I could mention your name if you'd like."

Tracy's heart lifted at this stroke of luck. She told him about Bob's call.

"I'll talk to my boss. Why don't you meet me for dinner around six and I'll let you know what he says?"

Tracy agreed. She went home and took a shower. She was so excited that things seemed to be going her way that she put on her favorite dress and earrings. She arrived at the small family owned Italian restaurant where she had agreed to meet Tom at six.

Tom was already sitting at a table. He stood when he saw Tracy. "Come and sit down. I ordered us a bottle of Cabernet."

"How was your meeting?" she asked nervously.

"The position is still open. My boss can meet with you tomorrow if you're available."

"That would be great. Thank you so much. I was beginning to think I would have to give up and go back to Ohio."

"I bet Ray would have been happy about that."

She told him about her fight with Ray. "Sometimes, he just doesn't get it."

"I know how you feel. Debbie and I had the same problem."

As they ate their lasagna and continued talking Tracy thought *Tom and I have a lot in common*. She found herself baring her soul like she would with Stacey, Becca, or even Ray. As the evening went on and she found herself enjoying Tom's company more and more, a feeling she couldn't quite place began nagging at her. *It's guilt. I feel guilty about having such a great time with Tom when I should be trying to work things out with Ray.* By the time the waiter asked if they would care for dessert or coffee Tracy was feeling nauseous. She told Tom that she had better get home, but she would see him the next day at the interview.

When she got home, she immediately called Ray. She told him how much she loved him and how sorry she was about the fight.

"I'm sorry, too."

She asked if he could hold off coming to California just a little longer and then told him about the interview planned for the next day.

"That's great, Trace. Where did you hear about it?"

She hesitated for a moment before she answered. "Tom told me about it."

"I don't remember you mentioning anyone named Tom."

"I told you about him, Ray. He was the head of operations at my old company."

"Yeah, I vaguely remember something about that. So what, did he just call you out of the blue to offer you a job?"

Tracy could feel another fight brewing, but knew it would be worse if she didn't tell him the whole truth. *Why didn't I tell Ray about running into Tom at the beach the other day?* As she started to explain about her unplanned meetings with Tom, she could hear the silence on the other end of the phone getting louder.

"Can I ask why you've been spending all this time with this guy and you haven't mentioned it before now?"

"It didn't seem that important at the time. I was so excited about the job at PAK, and then we got into that stupid fight."

"Tell me, Tracy. What was that fight really about? Why don't you want me to come to LA? Is it really because of this job business or are you just worried that if I come out there you won't be able to spend as much time with Tom?"

"You'd better stop, Ray, before you say something that you regret."

"Well, then I guess I'd better get going."

"Fine."

"Fine." All Ray heard on the other end was a dial tone.

Chapter 10

Ray hung up the phone slowly. *What is wrong with me? I trust Tracy. She would never cheat on me. This Tom is probably a good guy. And it's nice of him to help Tracy get a job.* Ray knew that this fight had nothing to do with Tom. It happened because he felt guilty that when Tracy asked him to wait to come to California he felt more relief than disappointment. As much as he missed Tracy, life in Chardon was going pretty well. The job at the high school was rewarding and fun. He was getting a kick out of watching the romance bloom between Becca and the new diner owner, Matt. And even though he was loyal to Tracy, he had noticed that the girls in town were acting a little bit different since she wasn't around. It was no big deal, just a little innocent flirting. Denise, one of the teachers at the school, had brought him a plate of cookies. And when he stopped at the diner, the ladies would invite him to sit with them in a booth instead of at the counter by himself. Ray hated to admit it, but he was enjoying the attention.

Ray realized that he was pacing. *I've got to get out of here.*

He got in the car and drove. He wasn't sure where he was going, but found that the car took him straight to the diner. He walked in and saw Becca. She smiled and waved.

"Coffee, Ray?"

He nodded and she brought over a steaming cup. "What's with you? You look like you lost your best friend."

"Tracy and I had a fight."

"Listen, I was just about to take my break. Give me a couple minutes and you can tell me all about it."

Becca took care of her last few tables, got herself a cup of coffee as well as refilling Ray's, and sat down.

Ray began spilling his guts. He talked for fifteen minutes, becoming more upset the longer he spoke. "I don't know if I gave her such a hard time because I feel so guilty about enjoying the attention from the other girls or if it was because I was hoping she wouldn't find another job. And then she would come home and we could get married and raise our family here. I've just got to face it, the fight was my fault." He crossed his arms on the table and laid his head down.

"Ray, it takes two to fight. Don't beat yourself up so much. So you enjoy the attention from the other girls, you've always been loyal to Tracy and everyone around here knows it.

"And don't feel guilty for wanting to raise your family in Chardon. Everybody you know and love is here. Your kids would have the same teachers you had when you were in school; they would play in the same parks. I really think Tracy would come to the same conclusion given enough time."

"That's what I think, too. But what if she doesn't?"

"There's never a guarantee. But look at me for example. I spent so many years pining for you that I never gave another guy the time of day. When Tracy left and we started spending more time together, I realized how different we are and how perfect you are for Tracy. As soon as I let go of my obsession with you, I was free to meet Matt and fall in love. I even discovered a new appreciation for the diner. All these years I've been so focused on how much I hate waiting on customers, I never realized that I love to cook. Spending time with Matt, helping him set up the new prep area and bakery and working on new recipes has been a blast. I always thought I needed to get out of Chardon to find my life's work. Instead I just needed to try something new.

"Did you know that when Matt asked me out I had my two week's notice in my apron pocket? At the time I thought I was leaving the diner and Chardon to find my destiny. Now I realize I was running away from my destiny. I guess the question is who is running from their destiny, Tracy or you?"

Ray didn't have an answer.

"I should get back to work. I'll call you tomorrow and we can talk some more. Or call me later tonight if you need to."

"Thanks for being such a good friend," he said as he gave her a hug. "I'm glad you found happiness with Matt. You deserve it."

As he left the diner he thought to himself, *I'm so confused. What am I going to do?*

Chapter 11

Ever since Tracy left the midnight hour is the longest one. Ray sat on the hood of his car looking at the overpass in the headlight's beam. As he stared at the words fading from the Midwest rain and the summer sun he relived every important moment with Tracy.

The first time he saw her . . . She was four, he was five. She was in overalls and pigtails playing in the sandbox. She shared her shovel with him.

Asking her out for the first time . . . Terrified she would say no. Her smile as he tripped over his words. His elation when she said, "I'd love to."

Their first date . . . Miniature golf. She won by five strokes. Sharing funnel cake. The wind blowing powdered sugar on them.

Their first kiss . . . Four dates later she finally let him kiss her. He could remember everything about that moment. The Righteous Brothers' "Unchained Melody" playing on the radio. The way her hair smelled. Her breath on his face. The touch of her lips.

The first time she said "I love you."

Going off to college.

Moving into the apartment.

The first time he saw the overpass.

The recent fights.

Ray came to a decision. He would call Tracy and they would work this out. Whatever it took. If she needed him to wait to go to California, he would wait. If she wanted him to come now, he wouldn't even pack a bag, he'd get on the first flight. He wanted to go home and call her, it was only 9:00 p.m. in California. But he knew that Tracy would have gone to bed early in preparation for her big interview. *I'll bet she went to that diner for dinner, had a root beer float, went home and took a long bath, and went straight to bed.* Ray leaned back against the windshield and spent another hour staring at the words on the overpass.

༶༶༶

Tracy's interview was supposed to be first thing in the morning. Where could she be? It was 8:00 p.m. in Ohio and Ray was getting worried. He had been trying to call since 4:00 p.m. *Maybe it didn't go well.* He realized that for the first time, the prospect of Tracy not getting the job did not make him happy. *I want her to get the job. She deserves it.*

An hour passed and he grew more and more worried. Was she not answering the phone because she knew it was him calling? Would she let him explain how sorry he was for being a jerk if he did get through? He realized just how important Tracy was to him. *Without Tracy, nothing else is worthwhile.*

He called Stacey and Becca to see if they had heard from her. No one answered at Stacey's apartment and he had left several messages for Becca with her mother. By the time she returned his calls around 10:00 p.m. he was starting to panic.

"I have to go to LA, Bec. I'm going crazy. I need to see her. I need to hold her. I booked myself on the first flight in the morning."

"Well, it sounds like you figured out what you want."

"I want Tracy. She's all I ever wanted."

Chapter 12

Late the next morning, Ray flew from Cleveland to LA. As the plane was landing at LAX, he realized he had no idea what to expect. Would he stay forever, would he leave alone? In the cab on the way to her apartment he could barely contain his excitement. He ran up the stairs and knocked on the door. No answer. He sat down on the steps. *I've waited for months for our reunion; I can wait a few more hours.* Half an hour later a man approached.

"Can I help you? Are you here to see the apartment?"

"No, I'm here to see Tracy. She lives in this building. I flew in from Ohio, but she doesn't seem to be home right now."

"You must be Ray. I'm Jay, the superintendent of the building. I've been off the past few days, but I did see her this morning when she returned her key. She was in quite a rush. I'm afraid she didn't mention where she was going. All she said was to wish her good luck in her new job. From the way she talks about you, I find it hard to believe she didn't tell you she was moving."

"Things have been kind of rough for us lately. That's why I'm here." After a few minutes of conversation, Ray shook Jay's hand. "Thanks for the information."

∽∾∾∾∾

Ray had no idea what to do next. He could call Michele or Tom, but he didn't even know their last names. *Why did I have to be such a jerk? She was probably home all day yesterday packing and didn't answer the phone because she knew I was the one calling.*

Ray began roaming the neighborhood. She had described all of her favorite places in such detail that it was as if he could feel her presence at each one. He searched the art galleries and parks. He found the diner that Tracy said reminded her of Jimmy's. The owner said she came in often, but he hadn't seen her recently.

Just before sunset he went to the beach, but Tracy wasn't there either. He plopped down in the sand with a grunt of defeat. He put his head in his hands and closed his eyes. *There's got to be somewhere else to look. There's got to be something else I can do.* He could see the overpass with its declaration "Tracy loves Ray." The far off whining of an engine caught his attention, he opened his eyes, looked up to the sky, and knew what he had to do.

Ray grabbed a pizza and headed back to the apartment building to take Jay up on his offer to put him up for the night. As the two bonded over pizza and beer, Ray told Jay about his plan.

"Unfortunately, I only can afford to do it once. I just pray that Tracy will see it."

Jay grabbed the telephone. "I have a friend who may be able to help you, let me give him a call."

꧁꧂

Early the next morning Ray was back on the beach, his eyes focused on the sky. Each hour he watched as the plane flew by and wrote "Ray Loves Tracy" in great big letters drifting in the air. *She'll call the phone number on the plane and they'll tell her to come to the beach. I just have to wait it out.*

As the day progressed he grew tired and depressed. It was after dark and there was still no sign of Tracy, so he gave up. He decided to go home.

Chapter 13

It was dawn. A new day was beginning, but Ray couldn't appreciate the sunrise. He had just landed in Cleveland on the red eye flight. He needed to get some sleep, but only after he called Becca and Stacey to see if they had heard from Tracy. As he drove home, the fight he had with Tracy replayed in his head. He wondered how he could ever make things right. He was driving fast, but when he made the turn onto Turner Road everything seemed to be in slow motion.

It has to be the glare of the sun. That's why it looks different.

In the dawn of the new day, the concrete seemed to shout "Tracy Loves Ray". *It has to be my imagination.* But it wasn't. The overpass was freshly painted in a frightening hue. He stopped the car and stared in disbelief. *What on earth am I doing? I have to get home.*

When Ray pulled into the parking lot he was so anxious to get up to the apartment that he forgot to take off his seat belt. "Argh!" he screamed. He unlatched the belt, jumped out of his seat, slammed the car door, and ran into the building. He took the steps two at a time and ran down the hall. He threw open the door and saw an empty living room. He ran into the bedroom, no Tracy. He checked the kitchen. *Where could she be?* Then he realized there was water running in the bathroom.

"Tracy?"

"Oh, Ray I missed you so much." She ran into the living room and threw her arms around him. They stood in the middle of the room holding each other for what seemed an eternity. When she pulled away, he took her face in his hands, looked deep into her eyes, and gave her the softest, sweetest kiss of her life. When they finally separated, he asked, "What are you doing here? I went to California, but you were gone. Jay said you got the job. Didn't it work out?"

"After I saw 'Ray Loves Tracy' written in the sky, I knew that I couldn't take the job. I knew I had to come home."

"But I came to California to be with you. I could have found a job. We could have raised a couple of beach bums."

"And they would have been cute beach bums, too," Tracy said. "LA was great and I think it would have been fun to raise our kids there. But LA doesn't hold a candle to Chardon.

"I know it took me a while to figure it out, but when I saw the skywriting everything became clear. Here I am sitting on the beach looking up at the sky laughing and crying at the same time. People must have thought I was nuts. I think some of them may have realized what I was looking at, but no one really knew what I was seeing.

"What I was seeing weren't the words 'Ray Loves Tracy' written in the sky, but the words 'Tracy Loves Ray' written on the overpass. And that's when I saw my future. I realized my future wasn't in California, it was here in Chardon; and our kids weren't bumming on the beach, they were swinging on the swings in Chardon Park and playing in the sandbox with their cousins and our friends' kids. I saw white Christmases, making snowmen and drinking hot chocolate. I saw you teaching history at Chardon High and leading the volleyball team to the championship. I saw the gang rooting you on to victory. I realized that I worked so long and hard to get away from this two-bit town, that I forgot how wonderful it really is. There is nowhere else on earth I'd rather be and I could never raise my family anywhere other than Chardon."

༄༅༄༅༄

The next day Ray and Tracy went to the overpass so he could repaint the faded "AND HE LOVES HER TOO." Instead he painted "TRACY WILL YOU MARRY ME?" She grabbed the spray can from his hand and painted "YES!" They were married three months later.

Chapter 14

"They were married three months later and they lived happily ever after. Until Tracy passed away, that is." Sunny choked on his final words. The diner was so silent that all that could be heard was the sound of coffee percolating. Tracy looked around at the adults. Most of them had tears in their eyes including her grandfather and Miss Becca. Tracy had lots of questions, but she thought that maybe now was not the best time to ask.

Miss Becca wiped the tears from her eyes and jumped up from her seat. "Who wants more coffee?"

Finny looked at his watch. "Look at the time. We're going to be late picking Gloria up at the airport. Say good-bye to everybody, Tracy."

Tracy made her way around the diner giving each man and Miss Becca a quick hug. When she got to Sunny she paused and said, "Thanks for telling me the Tracy Loves Ray story, Uncle Sunny. I'm sorry it made you cry."

"That's okay. We haven't told that story in a long time. Maybe even longer than you've been alive. It was time to tell it again."

"It sure was," Finny said putting his hand on Sunny's shoulder. "Tracy was great and we all loved her."

"Yes, we did."

And with that Finny and Tracy left the diner.

Chapter 15

A few weeks later, Tracy was helping her mother set the table for lunch. "Are you sure we can get Grandpa to go roller skating?" she asked.

"Honey, you have him wrapped so tight around your finger he'd probably wrestle a pig if you asked him. Oops, you better watch what you're doing; Grandpa's setting has two spoons and no knife."

Tracy fixed her mistake and double-checked that the rest of the table was set correctly. When the doorbell rang she ran to answer the door. "Happy birthday, Grandpa!"

Finny came in and exchanged hugs with his daughter and granddaughter. Hollis joined them and shook his father-in-law's hand. The group sat down and ate grilled Reubens, slaw, and fries. After lunch Finny opened his gifts. He was pleased to find a gift certificate to the diner from Hollis and Gloria and a new wallet from Tracy.

"Grandpa, will you go roller skating with us? Zach called earlier and said his whole family was going, even Matt and Miss Becca."

"I don't see why not. I don't have anything else planned for the afternoon."

"Great. Dad can drive. Right, Dad?"

"Sure, let's go."

The foursome climbed into the car and headed for the roller rink. Tracy asked her dad to drive by the overpass. "Pretty please, Dad, it's not that far out of the way."

"I suppose that would be all right. It looks like we're going to be early anyway."

Hollis made the right onto Turner Road and Finny let out a gasp. It seemed that half the town was standing in front of the overpass. When they got out of the car the crowd moved so Finny could see what young Tracy had done.

"TRACY LOVES RAY" the concrete screamed almost as loud as the day he had come back from LA.

"Tracy, how did you know? When you thanked Uncle Sunny I figured that you thought *he* was Ray." Tears were forming in his eyes.

"Silly, Grandpa. You should know better than to try to fool me."

"Actually, Tracy, you did think Uncle Sunny was Ray," Gloria reminded her daughter gently. She turned to address Finny. "She told us all about hearing the story at the diner and how bad she felt that it made Uncle Sunny cry. She said that it's sad that Tracy wasn't still here to paint the overpass for him. She was disappointed when we told her that Sunny wasn't the right Ray —"

Tracy interrupted her mother, "That's when I remembered Miss Becca telling me that Uncle Sunny was sad about his wife and sister dying in the same year. Well, Grandma was his sister. So, that meant that Grandma was Tracy and you must be Ray."

Gloria continued. "I was still debating whether or not you would be upset if I told her the truth when Tracy asked if you were Ray. A few days later she asked if she could paint the overpass for your birthday."

"It's beautiful, Tracy." Finny said as he picked her up and hugged her.

The group surrounding them began to applaud.

When the applause subsided, Finny said, "I can't believe you're all here. This is incredible."

Miss Becca stepped forward. "Gloria called me to let me know about the plan and I thought it would be fun if we were all here. It feels like our story, too."

Gloria said to Finny, "What I don't understand is how the story was told without even a mention that it's about you and Mom."

"I don't think it was deliberate. Maybe the guys thought I told her in the car when she saw the overpass and she already knew that it was about me. Somehow, it never came up."

"But why didn't you set her straight?"

"I hadn't been to the overpass since your mother passed away. Part of me honestly believed the words would have faded by now. I certainly wasn't expecting Tracy to notice it. So many emotions were tugging at my heart. I barely got through the telling of the story. I was so relieved that Tracy never asked who Ray was that I decided to let it go for a while."

"I'm surprised Mom didn't tell her the story when she was sick and Tracy would visit."

"I've thought about that, too. I think that it was such a part of our lives and our history it was almost like a habit. We didn't have to talk about it anymore. Each year your mother would paint the overpass and a day or two later I would paint 'AND HE LOVES HER TOO.' And that was that. It was just another part of us. A wonderful part, but no big deal. And then the year when she was sick, your mother had Becca paint it for her and I remembered just how much it meant."

Becca had brought several bottles of champagne. Matt started pouring and somebody turned on a radio. The crowd of townspeople were laughing and talking and crying. Finny was beaming, but inside he felt something was missing and he knew what it was. Dodger walked up and said, "I have a can of paint, if you're interested."

"You bet. I can't believe you remembered."

"I've been looking at that darn overpass for almost forty years. Of course I knew you would want to add 'AND HE LOVES HER TOO.' Now, I'll distract Tracy while you paint."

Finny worked quickly and was soon finished. As he waited for Tracy to notice, he walked over to Gloria. "It's a good thing Trickster was able to borrow the lift from the phone company because Tracy wanted to do all the painting herself," she was telling Becca.

"Just like her grandmother," Becca answered.

Finny interrupted, "Even with the lift it would have been hard for her to reach some of those high spots."

"I promised myself I wouldn't say anything, because you'll think I'm crazy. But there were a few moments when I felt Mom's presence. At one point I thought I saw Tracy lifted up to do the very top of the T."

"I don't think that's crazy at all," he whispered.

It was at this moment that Tracy noticed the addition to her message. She ran to hug her grandfather. Many of the onlookers began crying again. Becca cracked open another bottle of champagne and the group celebrated into the evening.

Hours later the party was winding down and there were only a few people left. Finny and Tracy were sitting together looking at the overpass.

He said, "You know, there are very few people in this world as lucky as me. Not only did an entire town show up to celebrate my birthday at an overpass, but they lived the story with me from start to finish. But you know the biggest reason I feel so lucky?"

"Because, we didn't make you to go roller skating?"

"No, but that's high on the list, too. Seriously, I am lucky to have had two Tracys in my life. How many people can say that they have been loved by one Tracy, let alone two?"

Chapter 16

Well, there you have it, the story of "Tracy Loves Ray." It's not the end though because the story lives on in the hearts and souls of the townspeople of Chardon. Becca has proposed that from now on Finny's birthday will include a celebration in honor of Tracy and Ray. Each year after young Tracy paints the overpass the Volleyballers will gather at Jimmy's Diner for Saturday brunch and a retelling of the story.

Since Finny's birthday a few months ago, not much has changed in Chardon. The holidays came and went. Dodger's daughter had twins and Newbie and his wife took a trip to Europe.

Sunny is a new person. Before the telling of "Tracy Loves Ray," he had fallen into a deep depression mourning both the loss of his wife and sister. The telling of the story to little Tracy allowed him to remember some of the good times without the heartache. And seeing the freshly painted overpass reminded him that even though his sister wasn't here to do the painting herself, she lived on in young Tracy, and his wife lived on in their children and grandchildren. Sunny became grateful for the time he had shared with those two wonderful women. He decided it was time to stop mourning them and to begin honoring them instead. He organized a pancake breakfast fund-raiser to benefit the American Cancer Society. It was such a huge success that they've decided to make it a yearly event.

Matt and Becca celebrated their thirty-second wedding anniversary right before Thanksgiving. They are looking forward to retiring in a few years and giving the diner to their daughter Susan and her husband Jeff.

Tracy began taking ballet and was in a dance class production of *The Nutcracker* during the holidays. She is doing well in school and even won a county wide spelling bee. One day for show and tell she took in a picture of the overpass and told her class the story.

Tracy's biggest news is that she became a big sister when her parents recently adopted four-year-old Kaleb. Finny gets a kick out of watching her answer her younger brother's never ending questions.

As for Finny, he's busier than ever. He is active in the session at church, babysits Tracy and Kaleb several times a week, and is helping Shawn build a new house.

A few weeks ago, he began volunteering at the information desk at the hospital. He figured this was a way he could give back to the doctors and nurses that had been so kind when his wife had been sick.

Even though he keeps busy by day, the nights are still hard. He misses Tracy's goodnight kiss and the warmth of her sleeping next to him. But now, when he feels lonely he closes his eyes and envisions the brightly painted overpass and the loneliness quickly subsides.

One thing that hasn't changed in Chardon and hopefully never will is that Saturday afternoons are for brunch and stories at Jimmy's Diner. In fact, it's about that time now.

Chapter 17

"Does anybody have any stories to share today? Or perhaps we would like to tell the 'Tracy Loves Ray' story," said Sunny on the Saturday after Finny's birthday surprise.

The men turned to Tracy expecting her to ask for "Tracy Loves Ray."

"Actually, I have some questions about my grandparents."

"Go ahead." Finny said.

"Well, if Grandma went to California for a job designing things and you were a history teacher, how did you end up running a sports store?"

"Your grandmother's job in California was in graphic design, which basically means you design pictures. When I decided to follow my dream and quit my job at the high school and open the sports store, your grandmother got the idea to design uniforms and banners for local sports teams. Her designs were so popular that teams came from towns all over Ohio to order from us."

"Tracy used to say, 'I went all the way to California to discover that my dream job was in Chardon.'"

Miss Becca added. "She and I are similar in that respect. It wasn't until I saw the town and diner through Matt's eyes that I realized how much I love it here."

When Tracy didn't say anything Finny asked, "Any other questions?"

"What about Grandma's friends from California? Whatever happened to them?"

"Your grandmother kept in touch with some of her west coast friends over the years. Jay continued to play his music. He eventually became successful enough to quit his job. Michele and Tom both married and raised their families in California.

"You may not remember meeting her, but Michele and her husband came to your grandmother's funeral, and several of her California friends flew out for our wedding. Our wedding, now there's a good story. Would you like to hear it?"

"You bet."

Chapter 18

Tracy was enjoying her last quiet moments with her bridesmaids while waiting for her brother Sunny to pick them up to go to the church. Tracy, Stacey, Becca, and Michele had been inseparable since Michele had flown in from California last week.

"It's been great getting to know you, Michele," said Becca. "I can't wait to meet Tom. It's just a shame that Jay couldn't make it for the wedding."

"Jay promised that he'll fly out for a visit as soon as he can," said Tracy. "Right now I'm more concerned about Sunny. He'd better get here soon. I don't want to be late for my own wedding."

"Maybe he lost track of time during the game. I'm sure he's on his way," said Becca. The guys had decided to play volleyball that morning to calm Ray's nerves before the wedding.

At that moment, Sunny came through the door. Tracy was surprised to see he wasn't in his tuxedo.

"Where have you been?"

"Tracy, I have some news you're not going to like."

"What's wrong? Is Ray okay? Is it Mom and Dad?"

"Everybody is okay, but there was an accident while we were playing volleyball and Ray broke his arm." Seeing the panicked look on his sister's face he continued quickly. "Everything's fine. They already set it in a cast and he'll be on time for the wedding. I'd better go put on my tux, so we're on time, too."

Sunny started to walk away, but turned back and said, "Ray says he loves you and he can't wait to marry you. And he hopes you're ready for a few surprises."

"Isn't a broken arm surprise enough?" she said, shaking her head in disbelief.

Twenty minutes later the five of them were in Sunny's car on the way to the church. It was an unusually warm day for January and the sun was shining bright. Tracy didn't notice the beauty of the day as she grew more nervous about being late. *Could Sunny find a longer way to go?* she thought to herself.

It wasn't until Sunny made a right hand turn onto Turner Road that she realized they weren't going to the church.

When she saw the overpass she said, "I can't believe it. How did he do this?"

"We did more than play volleyball this morning," said Sunny.

The guys had set up rows of chairs on the road in front of the overpass. There were vines entwined with flowers dangling from the overpass itself and a runner had been laid down the aisle where Tracy would soon walk to meet Ray to marry him. "It's beautiful," she whispered.

"Setting it up was the easy part. We got permission to close the road for the day, and because there were so many of us it only took fifteen minutes to set up the chairs. Mom and Mrs. Coleman took care of the flowers and the runner. The hard part was contacting the guests to tell them about the change of venue. Ray wasn't sure if the weather would hold out and he was also afraid that if he told people too early you would get wind of it and it wouldn't be a surprise."

"It's definitely a surprise."

The ceremony was simple. A few words from Reverend Leonard, the recitation of vows, and Tracy and Ray were married. There wasn't a dry eye when the minister pronounced them husband and wife and Ray kissed his bride.

As the crowd around them applauded, Ray put his unbroken arm around Tracy and whispered, "I have one more surprise," and Jay Hitt appeared strumming his guitar.

"Hello, everyone my name is Jay. Ray asked me here today to sing Tracy's favorite song for her. Instead I'd like to sing a song I wrote on the plane. I call it 'Tracy Loves Ray.'"

Jay began playing . . .

Tracy loves Ray, it must be so
I saw it on an overpass in Ohio
In great big letters so it must be true
It says Tracy loves Ray and he loves her too

Tracy got a job she couldn't turn down
She's moving to the City of the Angels now
Ray stays back till she settles in
He'll pack up the apartment and join her then
But distance never did a lover good
And time does things you never thought it would
She knows he'll miss her when she's far away
She leaves him a note he'll see everyday

Tracy loves Ray, it must be so
She wrote it on an overpass in Ohio
In great big letters so it must be true
It says Tracy loves Ray and he loves her too

"Tracy loves Ray," the letter starts
"From out on the west coast to deep in your heart"
But that company I work for is closing down
They told me today I'd better look around
She loves the ocean and the weather there
The California savoir faire
She sits on the beach and concentrates
On the boy that she left back in the Buckeye State

Tracy loves Ray, it must be true
She wrote it on the stone and she meant it too
But the sun comes up and the sun goes down
Tracy loves Ray but he's not around

Tracy loves Ray but she met a man
Just a couple of times there's nothing planned
Ray loves Tracy but the girls in town
Act a little bit different since she's not around
The midnight hour is the longest one
He never thought she'd be gone so long
And when his confidence is fading fast
He looks for the answers at the overpass

Tracy loves Ray in the headlight beam
Is disappearing, is washing clean
From the Midwest rain and the summer sun
It says Tracy loves Ray

Ray loves Tracy into LAX
He goes without knowing what he expects
Will he stay forever will he leave alone
He knocks on her door but she's not even home
The landlord says he knows she's not here
Cause Tracy's moved and he's no idea
One more chance, one more try
He hires a plane to write it in the sky

Ray loves Tracy in the LA blue
Everyone in Santa Monica knows it's true
Great big letters drifting in the air
Ray loves Tracy but she's not there

He lands in Cleveland on the red eye flight
Wondering how he'll ever make it right
Driving in to the breaking day
He sees it coming at him half a mile away

Tracy loves Ray the concrete shouts
In great big letters so there ain't no doubt
It's freshly painted in a frightening hue
It says Tracy loves Ray and he loves her too

Tracy loves Ray, it must be so
I saw it on an overpass in Ohio.

From song

To book

To movie

tracy

lo♥es

ray

A Love Story

Be a part of the story at tracylovesray.com

About the author - Theresa Child is a server and trainer at a restaurant in Pittsburgh, Pennsylvania. Over the years she has used her creativity and organizational skills to put together numerous birthday parties, baby and bridal showers, fundraisers, and church functions. In addition to being an active member of her church, Theresa runs a writer's group at a local library. In her spare time Theresa likes to visit her family's vacation home in Maryland, play Sudoku, and make cookies with her nephew. Tracy Loves Ray is her first novella.

About the songwriter - Jay Hitt has performed in many venues throughout the United States both as a solo artist and as a member of various bands. He has also written commercial music for radio advertising and a theme song for television. As a songwriter/arranger/performer Jay's musical versatility and down to earth folk style speaks to the listener of the simple joys found in everyday life. A talent for vivid storytelling combined with crisp and delicate acoustic melodies makes it easy to understand why Jay's songs so effortlessly touch the hearts of his fans.